# CHAPTER 1
## Super Duper News!

Cornelia skips into the house.

"I have super duper news!"

"Tell me," says Dad.

"Tomorrow is my one-and-only

show-and-tell day at school!" says Cornelia.

"I must bring something special and

unusual."

"Will you bring your rock collection?" asks Dad.

"No," says Cornelia. "Jason brought rocks."

"Will you bring your plastic horses?" asks Mom.

"No. Phoebe brought plastic horses," says Cornelia.

# Cornelia
## and the Show-and-Tell
# Showdown

by. Pam Muñoz Ryan

Illustrated by Julia Denos

Scholastic Inc.

New York   Toronto   London   Auckland

Sydney   Mexico City   New Delhi   Hong Kong

To Hope and Happ and Zellia.
— P. M. R.


For Matt P.
— J. D.

ISBN 978-0-545-15361-4

12  11  10  9  8  7  6  5  4  3  2        10  11  12  13  14  15/0

Printed in the U.S.A.                        40
First printing, January 2010

Book design by Jennifer Rinaldi Windau

"Will you bring me, me, me?" asks Peter.

Cornelia says, "Sorry, Peter. Marco already brought a little brother."

"What will you choose?" asks Dad.

"I have an idea," says Cornelia.

"Corny! Mr. Divine said to bring something special and unusual," says Cornelia.

Mom shakes her head. "I do not think school is a good place for a snake."

"A pet corn snake is unique," says Dad.

Mom says, "I will call the school for permission."

"I will go to the pet shop and buy a travel cage that is escape-proof," says Dad.

Before bedtime, Cornelia explains to

Corny about show-and-tell.

She reads him a story.

She sings his favorite song.

*One little snake went out to play,*

*out on a sunny rock one day.*

*He had such fantastic fun,*

*that he called for all his friends to come!*

Corny climbs to the top of his cage.

Cornelia tickles his tummy. "Sleep tight,"

she says. "Tomorrow is a big day."

# CHAPTER TWO
## Corny Goes to School

The next morning, Cornelia carries Corny into the classroom.

She puts the cage on the show-and-tell table.

The whole class crowds around the cage.

"Does he bite?" asks Phoebe.

"Only his food," says Cornelia.

"Is he poisonous?" asks Marco.

"Absolutely not," says Cornelia.

"Can I hold him?" asks Jason.

"Maybe later," says Cornelia.

Jason makes a face. "He looks slimy."

"Well, he isn't!" says Cornelia.

Mr. Divine peers into the cage.

"What colorful markings," says Mr. Divine. "And such bright eyes!"

"He's dazzling," says Cornelia. "Just like me."

"Of course he is! Can he get out of the cage?" asks Mr. Divine.

"No," says Cornelia. "It's escape-proof."

"Outstanding," says Mr. Divine.

Mr. Divine claps two times.

"Everyone in your seats," he says.

Cornelia whispers to Corny, "First there
is reading. Then math. Then after lunch is
show-and-tell. See you later, alligator."

# CHAPTER THREE
## Mad, Mad, Mad!

Mr. Divine is busy at the chalkboard.

Jason taps Corny's cage with his ruler.

He pokes his pencil through the holes in

the cage.

He makes silly faces at Corny.

Cornelia is steaming mad.

She crosses her arms.

She squints her eyes and stares at Jason.

But he does not stop.

Cornelia writes a note and passes it across the room.

It says: Stop bothering my snake!

Jason wads the note into a ball.

He throws it into the trash can.

He sticks his tongue out at Cornelia.

Cornelia raises her hand.

"Yes, Cornelia?" says Mr. Divine.

"Corny does not feel comfortable on the show-and-tell table. He prefers a sunny place," she says.

"You may put his cage on my desk," says Mr. Divine.

"Thank you," says Cornelia.

She picks up the cage and moves it.

On the way back to her desk, she glares at Jason and says, "It is not smart to be mean to a reptile."

my snake!

After lunch, it is time for show-and-tell.

Cornelia unlocks the cage and reaches inside.

She holds Corny up for everyone to see.

"This is Corny," she says.

"He is a corn snake. He likes to hide in tunnels and dark places. Once, he got lost in our car."

"Oh my," says Mr. Divine.

"But we found him the next morning," says Cornelia.

Everyone claps.

"He is strong, too," says Cornelia.

"Once, he opened the lid of his cage that had four books on top."

"Big deal," says Jason. He laughs and snorts like a pig.

The whole class laughs, too.

"That will be enough, Jason," says Mr. Divine.

Marco raises his hand. "Can we pet him?" he asks.

"Yes. But pet in the same direction as his scales," says Cornelia. "Like this."

She strokes Corny from the back of his head to his tail.

"And do not put your fingers near his mouth or he might think they are food," says Cornelia.

"You may pet the snake one at a time," says Mr. Divine.

Marco pets Corny. "He is a nice snake."

"The nicest," says Cornelia.

Phoebe pets Corny. "He isn't slimy at all," she says.

"I know," says Cornelia. "He's cool and smooth and silky."

"I like him," says Phoebe.

"He likes you," says Cornelia.

Next, it is Jason's turn.

Jason holds Corny in one hand.

He jabs a finger near Corny's mouth.

Corny flicks his tongue.

"Hey! I can make the snake stick out its tongue!" says Jason.

"Stop!" says Cornelia.

24

Jason laughs and pokes at Corny again.

Corny flicks his tongue out and in, out and in.

"Stop right now!" says Cornelia. "He doesn't like that!"

Jason does not listen.

He starts to tap Corny for a third time.

But Corny has had enough.

# CHAPTER FIVE
## Snake! Snake! Snake!

Corny darts toward Jason's finger.

Jason jerks away and stumbles backward.

He trips and falls.

Corny lands on Jason's chest.

Jason is nose-to-nose with Corny.
**"Aghhhhhhh!"** wails Jason.

Jason tosses Corny into the air.

"Noooooo!" shouts Cornelia.

Corny lands on the pillows in the book nook.

He slides down the pillows and slithers fast across the floor.

Cornelia leaps over Jason. "Corny, come back!" she cries.

Phoebe screams.

Marco trips over the crayon bin.

Jason jumps on top of a desk.

Everyone squeals, "Snake! Snake! Snake!"

Mr. Divine shouts, "Stay calm! Stay calm!"

But no one is calm.

# CHAPTER SIX
## Let's Find Corny

Mr. Divine claps twice, but no one hears

him.

Finally, he stands on a chair and points to

the door.

"Everyone outside," he yells.

All of the children rush out of the room, except Cornelia. She sniffles. "My pet is missing."

Mr. Divine takes a deep breath.

"Cornelia, let's find Corny."

Cornelia searches inside every desk.

Mr. Divine looks in every cubby.

The door opens a crack.

Phoebe comes inside.

"May I help?" she says.

"Aren't you scared?" asks Cornelia.

"No," says Phoebe. "It wasn't Corny's fault.
And Corny is the one that must be scared."

"Yes," says Cornelia. "He is probably
terrified."

Cornelia and Phoebe flip through the

papers in the homework basket.

Mr. Divine opens the class's lunch bags.

Marco opens the door and peeks inside.

"Can I help, too?" he asks.

"Yes, please," says Cornelia.

"Explore every backpack," says Mr. Divine.

One by one, almost everyone comes back
into the classroom to look for Corny.

"Cornelia, is there anything that might encourage Corny to come out of hiding?" asks Mr. Divine.

Cornelia pats her face and thinks and thinks.

She holds up a finger.

"He has a favorite song."

*One little snake went out to play,*

*out on a sunny rock one day.*

*He had such fantastic fun,*

*that he called for all his friends to come!*

# CHAPTER SEVEN
## Outstanding Day

"There he is!" says Cornelia. She picks him up and tickles his tummy.

"Outstanding!" says Mr. Divine. "Cornelia, please put Corny back in his cage."

He claps his hands twice. "Everyone else, back in your seats."

The door inches open.

Jason comes back into the classroom.

Mr. Divine says, "Jason, you are very lucky that Corny did not nibble on your finger. Now, sit down and write a paragraph on the proper way to handle a snake."

"Yes, Mr. Divine," says Jason.

"Afterward, if it is all right with Cornelia, then you may hold Corny," says Mr. Divine.

"Maybe some other time," says Jason.

Jason passes Cornelia's desk. "Sorry," he mutters. "I hope Corny is okay."

Cornelia is still mad at Jason. But he did say he was sorry. She sits a little taller. "I will pass your feelings along to Corny."

Dad and Peter meet Cornelia and Corny after school.

"Good-bye, Corny!" calls Phoebe.

"Come back soon!" says Marco.

"It sounds like show-and-tell day went well," says Dad.

"It was outstanding," says Cornelia.

"Did Corny make friends, friends, friends with everyone?" asks Peter.

"Well," says Cornelia, "almost everyone."